The Hessian's Secret Diary

by Lisa Banim
Illustrated by
James Watling

SILVER MOON PRESS
NEW YORK

First Silver Moon Press Paperback Edition 1998

Copyright © 1996 by Lisa Banim

For information contact:
Silver Moon Press
New York, NY
(800) 874-3320

Library of Congress Cataloging-in-Publication Data

Banim, Lisa, 1960-
The Hessian's Secret Diary/by Lisa Banim.
p. cm. —(Mysteries in Time series)
Summary: During the summer of 1776, ten-year-old Peggy discovers
a wounded soldier in the woods near her Brooklyn farm, and is
convinced that his sketchbook contains the secret notes
of a Hessian spy.

ISBN 1-893110-00-1 $5.95
1. Brooklyn (New York, N.Y.)—History—Revolution,
1775-1783—Juvenile fiction.
[1. Brooklyn (New York, N.Y.)—History-Revolution, 1775-1783—
Fiction.] I. Watling, James, ill. II. Title III. Series: Mysteries in Time
PZ7.B2253He   1996
[Fic]—dc20
96-757
CIP
AC

10 9 8 7 6 5 4 3 2 1

Printed in the USA

To Stephanie St. Pierre

1

Brooklyn, New York, August 1776

TEN-YEAR-OLD PEGGY VAN BRUNDT pushed back her white cotton cap and wiped her damp forehead as she stared out the window. August was always hot and muggy, but this summer was even worse than usual.

This summer was worse for another reason, too. Peggy used to spend the long, sunny days in her own special place in the woods, not far from her family's small, white farmhouse. Other summers, after she had finished the morning chores, Peggy would call her dog, Patches, and run to the woods. The best part was wading barefoot in the cool water of the shallow brook. There the two of them would chase frogs and hunt under rocks for crayfish.

But this summer everything was different. Mosquitoes were spreading a terrible disease called malaria. There had even been a few cases of the deadly smallpox. Worst of all, Peggy had heard grown-ups saying that a terrible battle was brewing. For weeks British ships had been arriving in the harbor. The woods in Brooklyn were said to be full of Continental soldiers under the command of General George Washington.

"Mother, please can't I go outside? Just

for a little while?" Peggy begged. It had been nearly a fortnight since her mother had let her out in the fields alone. It was bad enough being cooped up in the house and yard, doing dreary chores like feeding the chickens and churning butter. But now there wasn't even anyone to complain to. Peggy's older brothers, Willie and Jan, who were usually as eager to be done with their chores as Peggy, were spending many of their days in the taverns across the river in New York. When they did come home, all they wanted to do was talk about taxes and battles. They and many of the Van Brundts' neighbors were angry at King George of England and his unfair rules.

"Please, Mother," Peggy tried again. She looked longingly out the window toward the meadow. It was filled with wildflowers and butterflies, and the sky was the same bright blue as a robin's egg.

"No, Daughter." Mistress Van Brundt playfully tugged on one of the long brown pigtails that stuck out from under Peggy's cap. "If I let you go, I would worry myself sick about your safety. Besides, your father and brothers will be home for an early supper tonight. Come and help me get it ready."

With a sigh, Peggy followed her mother to the kitchen. She knew her mother had been worried about many things lately, especially Willie and Jan. The boys were anxious to join up with the Continental Army. Peggy kept reminding herself to be extra helpful so her mother would have fewer burdens.

As they stepped into the kitchen, the heat hit Peggy's face. Feeling a bit dizzy, she slumped into the long bench next to the room's only table. There her mother had laid out the ingredients for the evening meal. A chicken was already roasting on a spit over hot coals in the large cooking fireplace. Her mother would turn it gently every few minutes. The coals hissed as hot fat dripped off the chicken. Mistress Van Brundt put on her long white apron and pushed up the sleeves of her dress.

"Come along, Margaret Anne," she said briskly, using her daughter's first name, "Help me roll out the pastry for the tarts. I will finish the rest of the meal myself. If you promise to be very careful, you may go outside, but just for a very short while. And you must stay near the big oak by the barn."

"Mother, couldn't I take a quick walk down to the brook instead?" Peggy asked. She took her apron from its peg on the wall and put it on, tying the long strings behind her back. Her ankle-length blue summer dress and petticoat peeked out just below the hem.

"Peggy, you know very well that there are men in the woods all around us. Goodness knows when they will pick up their muskets and begin a battle in earnest." Mistress Van Brundt shook her head. "I fear that as long as the King's soldiers remain in Brooklyn, you have to stay close to home."

"But..." Peggy began.

"Margaret Anne, if you continue with this pestering you will go nowhere at all." Mistress Van Brundt gave Peggy a stern look and handed her a bowl full of milk and eggs.

"Yes, ma'am," said Peggy. She beat a wooden spoon around in the bowl with all

her might until her mother raised one eyebrow. Peggy smiled at her weakly and hastily began beating the eggs more gently.

As she stirred the mixture in the big wooden bowl, Peggy gazed out at the meadow again.

Days earlier, she had watched from her bedroom window as red-coated British soldiers and blue-uniformed Hessians marched through her father's fields. The Hessians were soldiers from Europe, many of them German, who were paid by King George to fight in the colonies. Some of the men were on horseback. Some carried muskets and bayonets. A few were lugging huge, heavy cannon.

At first Peggy had found all of the activity exciting to watch, even though she knew that Patriot soldiers—many of them men and boys her family knew—might have to fight the King's men. But now Peggy wished all of them would just go away. She wanted her life to get back to normal. She wanted to get back to her special place.

Suddenly Peggy had dreadful thoughts: *What if those awful soldiers found it? What if they tromped around in their big heavy boots, stepping on frogs and bugs and crayfish? What if they crushed the wildflowers, dumped rubbish in the brook, and dug up the lovely moss that lined the banks?*

Peggy quickly added flour and salt to her bowl and mixed them into the milk and eggs. She was determined to return to the brook as soon as possible. As soon as the tart was done, she would have her chance.

She mixed even faster, and kept a careful eye on her mother. Soon Peggy was up to her elbows in the dough that she had made. After she smoothed out the pastry in a thin sheet, she used a metal round to cut it into small crusts. At last the tart pastries were ready to be filled.

"All right, Peggy," Mistress Van Brundt said finally. "You've earned a rest. Run on out to the yard if you'd like."

She smiled as Peggy tugged at her apron strings, nearly tearing them in her haste to get out of the hot kitchen. In a flash she was on her way out the door.

"Mind you, stay in the yard!" her mother called. But Peggy was already whistling for Patches.

The brown and black dog barked happily and sped ahead of Peggy toward the meadow. He seemed to know exactly where they were headed—and, just like Peggy, he couldn't wait to get there.

2

PEGGY PICKED UP HER SKIRTS AND RAN until her side began to ache. Finally she had to stop for a moment to catch her breath. She was more than halfway to the woods, but so far she hadn't seen any sign of soldiers. Glancing back over her shoulder, she thought that her family's farm looked as peaceful as it always had.

"Mother would be angry if she knew we were out here, but I just have to be sure everything is all right at the brook," Peggy told Patches.

The dog was happy to be out for a run. He jumped and barked and tugged at the hem of Peggy's dress. "All right, all right, you silly dog!" Peggy laughed. Patches seemed even more anxious than *she* was to get to the brook. He was probably very thirsty, too. "But we can't stay to play now," Peggy told him. "We will look around quickly and then go straight back home. We mustn't make Mother worry."

Patches barked in agreement and the two of them set off again.

As she skipped toward the woods, Peggy thought about her brothers. Much to their parents' dismay, Willie and Jan had recently declared themselves Patriots. They had even talked of joining the fight as soldiers themselves. So far, however, talk was all they had done. Peggy's father did not actually call himself a Loyalist, like some of their neighbors, but he was very much against the colonies' break with England and the war it was causing. He was worried that his farm would be ransacked—or worse, that he would lose his two strong sons. Life under King George wasn't perfect, but it hadn't been as much of a hardship for the Van Brundt family as it had been for others. Peggy herself didn't really understand what all the fuss was about.

But Peggy's brothers saw things in a different light. They were committed to the idea of freedom for the colonies. Across the river on Manhattan Island, they had heard rousing speeches in the streets and public houses, which they would, upon their return home, recite the next day for Peggy. They had even memorized the best parts of a proclamation that some colonial leaders had sent to King George. It was called the *Declaration of Independence.* It said that the colonies had declared themselves *"free and independent states."*

Freedom, Peggy thought, as she skipped and twirled through the field. *"Life, liberty, and the pursuit of happiness!"* Her special place always made her happy. And she certainly did feel free there. Surely her brothers would understand why she just had to go to the brook, soldiers or no soldiers.

It was well past noon now and the woods were shady. Peggy couldn't wait for a long, cool drink from the brook. Feeling a bit breathless again, she slowed her pace as she continued along the narrow path. There was still no sign of soldiers: Redcoat, Hessian, or Patriot. In fact, she didn't see anyone at all.

Finally Peggy and Patches arrived at the clearing around the brook. Their special place looked exactly the same as always.

"Oh, Patches, everything is just fine!" Peggy exclaimed happily. She knelt down beside the brook and splashed the cool water on her face. Then she took a refreshing drink and lay down, pleased and exhausted, on the mossy bank.

At least nothing seemed to have been trampled by the troops traveling through. Peggy couldn't help wondering how long it would be until the big battle everyone feared finally began. *Would the soldiers fight in this very place?*

The Patriots had been building earthworks and forts around the harbor and all around Brooklyn to protect the area. That's what Peggy's brothers had told her, anyway. And though the colonists had won some major battles against the Redcoats up in Massachusetts just a short time ago—even driving the British soldiers from the city of Boston—they would have a very difficult time doing so in New York. Everyone knew that if the British could control Manhattan Island and the Hudson River, the colonies would be divided. That would make the Patriots' fight for freedom much harder.

Patches took a long, noisy drink and then nuzzled Peggy with his wet nose.

"Get away from me!" Peggy laughed. "You're getting my dress all wet! What will Mother say?"

Patches didn't look one bit sorry.

"It wouldn't hurt to do one little sketch before we go back home, would it?" Peggy asked her dog. He wagged his tail and licked her cheek. "All right, then." She patted Patches on the head and pulled out the small, old sketchbook that she always carried in her pocket. Mister Van Brundt had once used it to keep accounts for the farm. A small stub of charcoal was stuck between the pages, wrapped in a square of cloth so it wouldn't smudge.

"Patches, sit!" Peggy said. The little dog immediately sat down and wagged its tail as she began to draw.

Besides Mister Van Brundt's scrawled numbers and notes, most of Peggy's sketchbook was already filled with half-finished sketches of Patches. They weren't very good, but she was getting better. Today she was working on the ears. She

could never seem to get them just right. "Don't move," she told the restless little dog. "This will take just a minute, I promise."

3

PEGGY CONCENTRATED AS HARD AS she could on Patches's ears. She was beginning to get them right—until Patches suddenly twitched his ears back.

Peggy frowned. "Didn't I tell you to stay still?" she said. "Now we're going to have to start all over again."

Almost immediately, Patches stood up.

"Sit!" Peggy said sharply. She pushed against his backside. But Patches did not sit down. He turned toward the woods and stared. He took a step forward.

Just then, Peggy was startled to hear a low growl. She looked around fearfully. Was there an angry animal in the woods? But she realized that the growl had come from Patches.

"What is it, boy?" Peggy whispered. She was beginning to get worried. Patches never growled. But there was no other sound or movement in the woods.

Patches continued to stand at attention. Finally, Peggy heard a rustling sound in the brush a few feet into the trees. "It's probably just a squirrel," she said quietly. Still, Patches was used to squirrels and other small animals. He never growled at them.

Quickly, Peggy shoved her sketchbook into her pocket and stood up. "Come on, Patches. We're going home now."

Suddenly, the noise grew louder—too loud to be made by anything as small as a squirrel. Patches barked sharply and took off at a run.

"Fiddlesticks," Peggy said. She hesitated for just a moment, then followed Patches into the brush. "Patches, come back here!" she called. *"Patches!"*

Peggy ran further into the woods, but she soon lost sight of the little brown and black dog. As she ran, branches caught at her dress and she heard the cloth tear. *How will I explain this to Mother?* Peggy wondered. But she kept running. Maybe Patches was after a deer. *A soldier certainly wouldn't be sneaking around in the woods, at least not running.* That thought made Peggy feel less afraid.

"Patches, wait, you naughty dog!" Peggy cried. She heard a sharp bark and hurried in the direction of the sound.

Following her dog's excited barks, Peggy pushed through a thicket of evergreen bushes. Finally, she spotted Patches. He was tearing madly around in circles, sniffing. Every now and then he stopped and barked. He seemed to have lost whatever it was he'd been tracking.

"Some hunter!" Peggy scoffed. "I guess I wasn't the only one who couldn't keep up!"

The little dog trotted over to her, then looked around and stopped barking.

"It's gone, Patches. Let's go." Peggy was about to give up and head for home when she spied something in the mud nearby.

"What's this?" She walked over and bent down to get a closer look.

"Footprints!" Peggy gasped. "So you really were after something, Patches." The marks had definitely been made by someone wearing big boots. *A soldier?* she wondered. But why would a man with a musket have run away from a young girl and a dog?

One thing was certain, Peggy thought, *he couldn't have gone far.* That meant the person was still around somewhere. Maybe he was even watching from some nearby hiding place. Could the man be a spy?

A shiver ran down Peggy's spine. Her brothers had told her about spies. "Come on, Patches," she said. "We're going home."

But even though Peggy was frightened, she couldn't help being curious.

She walked around the clearing to the spot where she'd first seen Patches sniffing and barking. There were a few faint footprints and the grass had been crushed, but the trail ended here. There was no telling where the mysterious stranger had gone. He had most likely gone to the brook to get a drink of nice, cool water. Perhaps he would return there again.

And if he does, I'll be looking out for him, Peggy thought grimly. She'd already made up her mind.

She would return to the brook again tomorrow and do some spying of her own.

4

"MARGARET ANNE VAN BRUNDT! How ever did you manage to tear your new summer dress?" Mistress Van Brundt stood with her arms folded across her chest frowning at Peggy. Peggy was sitting under the big oak tree, trying to look as though she'd been there all afternoon. Except for the tear in the hem of her dress, there was nothing to tell her mother that she had been up to any mischief.

Peggy looked down at the tear. "Ummmm, I don't know," she said in a small voice.

"Well, never mind," said Mistress Van Brundt with a sigh. "Come inside now and help me lay the table. Supper is nearly ready. Your brothers were asking for you."

At the mention of her brothers, Peggy jumped up eagerly and ran to the house.

"Willie! Jan!" she called.

"In here," a voice called back.

Peggy entered the parlor. Her brothers were sitting in the two big wooden chairs, sharing news from New York with their father.

"Hello, Father," said Peggy. She ran to give him a peck on the cheek.

"Good day, Daughter. Where have you been?" Mister Van Brundt asked. "Your mother was about to send your brothers out searching."

"I'm fine, Father," Peggy said. She hoped her cheeks weren't turning red as they usually did whenever she told a fib. "Patches and I were just playing."

She ran over to give both of her brothers a hug. Then she returned to the kitchen to help her mother get supper on the table.

She was determined to try to learn more from her brothers about spies during the meal. She needed to prepare for tomorrow, when she and Patches would return to the woods.

THE NEXT MORNING, PEGGY was up bright and early. She hurried to finish her regular chores. Then she asked her mother if she needed her to do anything more.

"Why, I can hardly believe my ears," Mistress Van Brundt said. "Is this really my Peggy?"

"Mother," Peggy said, frowning. "I am ten years old now. I have learned to be very responsible."

"I see," said Mistress Van Brundt with a smile. "Well, come and help me with the mending. Then perhaps you can have some time to yourself."

Peggy groaned silently. Mending was her *least* favorite chore.

"And the first thing you can mend is the dress you tore yesterday," her mother added.

It was a long morning, but finally the work was finished.

PEGGY AND PATCHES STARTED through the meadow once again. This time Peggy kept an even sharper eye out for signs of anyone who might be lurking in the woods.

When they reached the path that led to their special place, Peggy held Patches back by his collar.

"Quiet, boy," she whispered. "Let's see if we can catch that spy today. We can hide in the brush near the brook and wait until he comes for a drink of water. He'll have to, if he's still around here."

They had nearly reached the brook when Peggy suddenly stumbled on a tree root and let go of Patches' collar for just a moment. Immediately, the little dog took off at a run, growling and barking.

"Wait!" Peggy cried, and ran after him. Moments later, she burst into a clearing near the brook—just in time to see a ragged-looking stranger hurry away.

Peggy stopped dead in her tracks. She wasn't sure what to do next. She hadn't actually planned what to do once she *found* the spy.

She moved closer to Patches. The dog was waiting near the edge of the brook, barking at the spot in the woods into which the mysterious stranger had disappeared.

Who could the person be? Peggy wondered. She was quite certain of one thing: He had to be a spy. Why else would he sneak around like this in the woods?

Peggy tried to remember every detail of the person she had glimpsed. She hadn't seen his face, but he had brown hair and was wearing a torn coat. It might have been a uniform, but it was too dirty to tell what color it had been.

She looked down and saw several sets of footprints at the muddy edge of the brook, all of them the same. They seemed to be about the size of those she had found yesterday, made by big heavy boots. They

could very well belong to the same person.

Patches barked sharply twice.

"Shh," Peggy told him. "He's gone now." She patted the dog until he seemed reassured, but she was feeling a bit nervous herself. "Maybe we should get home before Mother notices we're not in the yard."

Just then, Peggy spotted an object lying in a patch of sunlight a few fect away.

To her surprise, the object was a small leather-bound book. It was lying open on the soft mossy spot where Peggy liked to sit and sketch.

Peggy picked up the book. The open page was covered with writing in a strange language she could not understand.

But to Peggy, the most interesting thing about the book was the artwork. The open page showed a nearly finished drawing of the very clearing in which she was standing.

It was a perfect likeness.

She flipped to another page and found sketches of other places she recognized from the farm and the nearby town. There was even a sketch of the New York Harbor and the tall ships anchored there. All of the pages contained little notes scribbled in that odd language.

Patches brushed against Peggy's legs, reminding her that they should get home. She snapped the book shut and stuffed it into her pocket beside her own more humble sketchbook. Maybe she should show her findings to Willie and Jan. Perhaps her brothers could tell if it was a spy's handiwork. She would tell them the whole story tonight if they returned from Manhattan Island before she fell asleep.

But for now, Patches was the only one who would share her secret.

5

PEGGY AND PATCHES WERE NEARLY halfway home to the farmhouse when they heard a loud *boom!*

At first, Peggy thought it was thunder. But even though the wind was picking up a bit, there wasn't a storm cloud in sight. The sky was cloudless and blue. The sound came again, faster and louder. *Boom, boom, BOOM!* Whatever it was, it wasn't far away.

Maybe it's cannon fire! Peggy thought in alarm. Could the long-awaited battle have begun?

Now she was really frightened. Picking up her skirts, Peggy ran as quickly as she could toward the barn.

Patches didn't like those loud sounds, either. He streaked ahead of Peggy and disappeared. Peggy figured he was hiding in the hayloft. That's where he usually went during thunderstorms.

The booming grew louder as more cannon—and muskets—were shot. Peggy thought she could hear shouting, too. At any moment she half expected to see the battle looming in front of her. It felt that close.

Peggy kept running until she reached the barn. Her heart was pounding and she could barely catch her breath. As she slowed her pace and rounded the corner, she was relieved to see her father.

"Father!" she cried out.

Mister Van Brundt ran to Peggy and pulled her close. She knew she would get a scolding later, but her father was too happy to see her safe to lecture her now. Together they went into the house.

"Peggy!" Mistress Van Brundt nearly crushed Peggy in her arms when she saw her daughter come through the door. "Where were you? What happened? Oh, I am so glad my little girl is safe."

Tears began to stream down Peggy's face. "I'm sorry, Mother," she said. She was still feeling frightened, and she had never meant to cause any trouble. "Patches and I only went for a short walk. I'm so sorry."

"Well, thank goodness you are safe," said Mistress Van Brundt. At last she let

Peggy go. "We'll have some tea and johnny-cakes," she said, and hurried off to the kitchen.

Peggy watched her go in surprise.

Mister Van Brundt came over and placed a hand on Peggy's shoulder. "Your mother needs to keep herself busy right now," he said. "I fear she is very worried about Willie and Jan."

"Do you think they are in the fighting, Father?" Peggy asked.

"I don't know." Mister Van Brundt frowned. He looked quite worried himself. "We can only watch and wait and pray until the battle is over."

Peggy walked over and stood by the window. She could still hear the cannon booming, but everything outside looked the same as always.

Near nightfall, Mister Van Brundt left to

check on the animals in the barn. Peggy wanted to go with him and look for Patches, but she didn't even ask. She knew she would not be allowed out of the house. Mistress Van Brundt was in the kitchen, preparing another meal in case the boys returned in the middle of the night. Peggy had a feeling her mother wanted to be by herself for a while, too.

The noise of battle had finally begun to die down with the setting sun, but the air was heavy with gunpowder. In the distance, clouds of black smoke were rising. Perhaps one of the nearby farms was on fire. Peggy felt sad for her neighbors, but she couldn't help feeling grateful that her own family's home was still safe.

She searched the darkening sky until she found what she was looking for: a wishing star. When she found one she whispered, "Let my brothers be safe and sound and come home soon!"

Suddenly, she remembered the stranger's sketchbook. In all the excitement of the afternoon, she had forgotten all about it. Digging deep in her pockets, she pulled out the book. Then she lit a candle on the table and began to look at the beautiful drawings again. *This artist is much more skilled than I am,* she thought.

Just then, a sudden commotion began outside. Peggy looked out the window again and saw a small group of British soldiers nearing her family's house. She could hear an officer on horseback shouting orders.

Mister Van Brundt emerged from the barn as the officers dismounted and approached the house. Peggy put down the sketchbook and ran to the front door

to listen from inside. She could barely make out the men's voices.

"I trust this house is loyal to the King, good man," the officer was saying. "No doubt you'll be happy to hear that the battle is over. Those ragtag Colonials were no match for His Majesty's men."

Peggy couldn't hear her father's reply. *Perhaps he said nothing,* she thought. *That is most unlike him.*

"Unfortunately, there are a few yellow-bellied deserters and spies that we have not caught up with yet," the officer continued. "You and your neighbors be warned. House-to-house searches will soon be conducted. Anyone found to be harboring enemies of the King will surely hang. If you see any suspicious lurkers-about or other scoundrels, they must be reported. My men will take care of any troublemakers."

Peggy gasped, thinking of her brothers. *Had they not declared themselves Patriots but a short time ago? Did that make them "troublemakers"? And what about the spy in the woods? Would her family be in danger because she hadn't told anyone about him?*

What should I do? Peggy thought frantically. She nearly threw open the door to blurt out her story to the officer, but something held her back. Then she heard more noises outside. The soldiers were leaving!

Peggy sighed and stepped back from the door. When her father entered, he looked more worried and tired than ever.

Peggy knew she couldn't trouble him with her secret now. She would have to tell him tomorrow. Perhaps by then her brothers would be home, safe and sound!

All she wanted was for this terrible day to be over.

6

IN THE MORNING PEGGY FELT BETTER. The cannon fire had stopped and even the sickening smell of gunpowder was gone. It seemed like another ordinary summer day. But it wasn't.

Peggy did her chores without a complaint. Willie and Jan did not come home at all the night before and everyone was worried. Her mother's eyes were red from crying. Her father kept pacing around the farmyard. It was awful not knowing what had happened to her brothers.

"Patches, I've got to find out who that man in the woods is," Peggy, intrigued by the mystery, whispered to her dog. "If he *is* a spy, we can tell Father. Then the British soldiers won't bother our family anymore."

Once again, Peggy planned to go back to the brook and watch for the stranger. She was sure he would come back for his sketchbook, especially if he was a spy. But how would she be able to sneak away from the house?

To Peggy's relief, that problem was solved when one of their neighbors, Mistress Josephs, arrived at the house with her three young children. She was afraid to stay alone at home while her husband rode to town to find out news of the battle. Peggy felt certain that the visitors would keep her mother occupied long enough for her to slip away and accomplish her mission.

Peggy decided to leave Patches at home this time. She didn't want him scaring the stranger away before she could get a good look at him.

"Come, Patches," said Peggy as she coaxed the dog into the old barn later that morning. She knew he wouldn't like being left behind, but she had saved some scraps from breakfast. Patches would be happy enough munching on them for a while.

Once the little dog was safely in the barn, Peggy gave him his treat. "Good boy," she told him, ruffling his fur. Then she was off.

On her way to the woods, Peggy saw several British soldiers. Some of them were on horseback, while others walked in groups. A few were limping, and Peggy could tell that they had been wounded in the battle. Luckily, they couldn't see her.

She continued on her way as though she hadn't seen anyone at all. She didn't want to be stopped before she could reach her special spot.

Peggy reached the woods safely and hid near the mossy bank where she liked to sit and sketch. It was the same place where she had found the sketchbook yesterday.

She waited and waited for what seemed like hours. She had nearly dozed off when a splashing sound jarred her back to attention.

Nervously, Peggy peered through the bushes. Sure enough, it was the mysterious stranger. He was leaning over the brook, drinking handfuls of water and splashing his face.

To Peggy's surprise, the stranger was a young man about the same age as Willie. His clothes were badly torn and she could see a huge, dark gash in one of his legs. *That wound must hurt a great deal,* Peggy thought.

The stranger drank for a long while, then splashed some water on the cut on his leg. Finally, he straightened and turned toward the spot where Peggy was hiding.

Can he see me? Peggy wondered, her heart thudding. *No,* she told herself after a moment. *He is only gazing at the spot where he lost his sketchbook.*

The young man began to limp slowly toward Peggy, his eyes still fixed on the ground. Peggy's heart beat even faster.

He came so close that Peggy could see his face quite clearly. He seemed very disappointed that he couldn't find his book.

Peggy felt a little sorry for him, even if he *was* a spy. He was mumbling to himself in a language that sounded familiar, but it was neither English nor Dutch.

The stranger seemed to grow nervous. It was almost as though he could sense Peggy watching him. He took one last drink from the brook and began limping back into the woods.

Peggy didn't know what to think. She did feel sorry for the young man because of the gash in his leg. She also knew how sad she would be if she lost her own sketchbook. She reached in her pocket and felt for the stranger's book.

Peggy suddenly realized a terrible thing. She had left the stranger's sketch-book on the windowsill last night when she had heard the soldiers outside talking to her father.

What if Mother and Father find it? Peggy thought, trying not to panic. Perhaps, if she ran very fast, no one would notice the sketchbook before she got home.

After all, Peggy told herself, the stranger might very well be a Patriot spy. He might even have been wounded by British soldiers. And if he was indeed a spy, the British would *hang* him if they caught him.

Peggy shuddered. The stranger was so young. He could have easily been a friend of Willie's. Peggy knew her mind would not be at rest until she knew who the stranger was. She would have to follow him, no matter how frightened she was.

It was easy for Peggy to track the stranger through the woods. Now that he wasn't trying to run away from her, he moved very slowly. His leg must have been very painful because he stopped often to rest.

Peggy racked her brain, trying to guess where the young man might be heading. Finally, the answer came to her: the old burned-out barn on the edge of her family's property. It was lonely but a good place to hide. She decided to slip ahead of the stranger and search the barn before he arrived. Maybe that way she could learn more about him to tell her father.

Peggy had just reached the field where the old barn was when Patches came bounding toward her, barking as usual.

"Shhhh!" Peggy whispered. By now she was far enough ahead of the stranger that he wouldn't hear her, but he might hear Patches. "Naughty dog. I should have known you'd dig your way out of the barn and follow me!"

The little dog jumped up and down, happy to have found Peggy. "All right," Peggy gave in finally. "You can stay, but be quiet!"

Patches stopped wiggling and barking and followed Peggy through the doorway into the barn. Two of the walls had been destroyed by the fire, but there was a corner of the barn still standing.

"That's where *I* would hide," she told Patches.

Sure enough, Peggy found signs that someone had been making the old barn his home. *Not a very comfortable home,* she thought. A pile of leaves served as a bed. A worn leather pouch lay on the floor, half hidden by leaves. Peggy was just about to reach for the pouch when Patches gave a low growl.

"You there!" a voice called sharply from

the barn's doorway.

Peggy stiffened. It was the stranger!

The young man said something else, but he had a thick accent and his words did not make sense to Peggy. There was no question about his tone, though. The stranger was angry.

Peggy stepped back from the pouch. The fur on Patches' back rose and he growled again, more fiercely.

"I'm sorry," Peggy said, trying to smile. She took a step forward. "Please, don't be angry. Perhaps I can help you."

The stranger didn't look angry anymore. He seemed as if he was about to reply, but suddenly he slumped against the doorway, his expression pained. He looked as though he might collapse on the floor.

Almost without thinking, Peggy ran to the young man's side. He drew back from

her at first, but finally he allowed her to help him over to the leaf pile. With a groan, he sank to the floor.

"Don't worry," Peggy told him. "You're going to be fine." But she could tell right away that the stranger had a high fever.

Patches was still growling. "Quiet, Patches," Peggy said. "Sit."

The little dog sat.

"I'm Peggy," she said to the stranger. He stared back at her, and she could see fear in his eyes. *No one has ever been afraid of me before,* Peggy thought. "Peggy," she repeated, pointing at herself this time.

To Peggy's relief, the young man nodded. "Me, I am Frederick," he said in a low, raspy voice.

"I will help you, Frederick," said Peggy. "I can bring you food. Do you understand?" Frederick nodded again. "And water, and some medicine for your leg."

"I must hide," Frederick spoke in a whisper. "Secret." He sounded very weak.

"I know," said Peggy. "I found your sketchbook." She made a motion with her hands as though she were opening a book and drawing, and Frederick's eyes lit up slightly. "I promise I'll bring the book to you. Until I can come back, you can use mine."

Peggy pulled her own shabby sketch-book from her pocket and handed it to Frederick. He hesitated for a moment, then opened it. Even though he was in pain, he smiled when he flipped through the drawings of Patches.

"These pictures, they are by you?" he asked.

"Yes," said Peggy, feeling herself blush. "But they're not as good as yours."

"They are enough good," Frederick

said. He closed the sketchbook and shut his eyes in pain.

"I have to go now," Peggy said quickly. "I'll come back with food and water and blankets as soon as I can."

"Our secret, no?" Frederick said. Peggy could see the fear returning to his face.

Peggy smiled and put a finger to her lips. "Our secret. I promise." Then she ran from the barn with Patches at her heels.

7

PEGGY STARTED HOME FEELING MORE confused than ever. Could Frederick really be a spy? She wasn't so sure now. He seemed like a kind person. And he needed her help.

If only Willie and Jan were home, Peggy thought with a sigh. Surely her brothers could help her figure out what to do.

Peggy decided she couldn't tell her parents—not yet. She was afraid she might endanger them if the British came back. It would be hard to get food and blankets and medicine out of the house unnoticed if they were already suspicious. She certainly hoped they hadn't discovered Frederick's sketchbook.

Peggy was still lost in thought as she approached the house. Suddenly, she looked up and stopped short, terrified. "Mother!" she cried. Mistress Van Brundt and Mistress Josephs and her children were huddled in the center of the yard. A British soldier with a musket stood at attention nearby. The children looked very frightened.

Peggy ran toward her mother. "What is it? What has happened?" she asked in alarm.

"These soldiers are searching all of the houses in Brooklyn, looking for spies and deserters," said Mistress Van Brundt nervously. "*Everyone* is being searched. The men will be done soon. Do not worry, Daughter."

"The sketchbook!" Peggy gasped, without thinking. She clapped her hand to her mouth. One of the British soldiers turned to frown at her, then he looked away.

"Is something wrong, Margaret Anne?" Mistress Van Brundt asked in a low voice.

"No, I mean, yes," Peggy whispered breathlessly. "I found something important in the woods and I left it on the windowsill last night. Where is Father? I must speak to him!"

"He's in the kitchen, Peggy. The lieutenant is asking him some questions."

"Oh, no!" Peggy cried in horror. She turned, ran toward the house, and burst straight into the kitchen.

Mister Van Brundt was seated in a wooden chair. He was surrounded by a group of angry-looking British soldiers holding bayonets. Frederick's sketchbook lay open on the table in front of him.

Peggy swallowed her fear. "Oh, you've found it, thank goodness!" she cried in a high, shaky voice. She ran to the table and reached for the book.

"One moment, young lady," said the lieutenant, frowning. He held his hand out to stop her from taking the sketchbook.

Mister Van Brundt stared at Peggy in surprise. "You have seen this book before?"

"It's *my* book," said Peggy. The lieutenant drew back, looking skeptical. "Oh, I didn't draw the pictures," she went on hastily. "I found it in the woods a few days ago. I thought the pictures were so pretty that I kept it. Was that wrong?" Peggy hoped her terror did not show in her voice.

Everyone in the room was staring at her now. Peggy's heart was beating wildly, but she did her best to look innocent.

"Are you aware, little maid, that the notes in this book are written in German?" asked the lieutenant.

Peggy opened her eyes wide. "Really? Oh, no. I thought all those marks were just scribbling. I'm not a very good reader."

The tension in the room seemed to lessen a tiny bit. The soldiers exchanged glances.

"Look at the pretty drawing of our house!" Peggy said quickly. She picked the sketchbook up from the table and flipped to one of the pages.

"Hmm," said the lieutenant slowly. "It is indeed an excellent likeness." He reached out and took the sketchbook from Peggy.

Then he turned to Mister Van Brundt. "My good man, it seems you spoke the truth when you said you knew nothing of this matter. I apologize for doubting your word. However, I trust you can understand my position." He turned back to Peggy. "I am afraid I must keep the sketchbook, miss."

Peggy tried to look as if she was very disappointed. It wasn't hard, because she did feel sad that she couldn't return the book to Frederick.

"This book may prove to be of no importance," the officer went on in a kinder tone. "But we must first be sure that it isn't the work of a spy."

"A spy?" Peggy gasped. Pretending that she might faint with fright, she reached for a chair to steady herself.

"There is nothing to worry about, little maid. The King's soldiers will keep you safe," the lieutenant said. "Come along, men." With a terse nod to Peggy and her father, he and his men left the room. Moments later, they galloped away on their horses.

Peggy sat down at the table across from her father. She was afraid to look at him. She had managed to save her family and the Josephs from terrible danger in the nick of time. The soldiers might very well have hauled Peggy's father off to a quick hanging. On the other hand, Peggy reminded herself, if it hadn't been for her carelessness, there wouldn't have been a problem in the first place. Now she had a lot of explaining to do.

And what about Frederick? Peggy wondered miserably. *What should she say about him? Should she try to help him, even if he was a spy? And how?*

8

"MARGARET ANNE, I AM VERY, VERY disappointed in you."

Peggy sat on a small wooden stool in a corner of the kitchen, her hands clasped in her lap. She was staring at the floor between her heavy brown shoes. Her father had already lectured her for disobeying her mother. Now, Mistress Van Brundt was scolding her.

"I am truly sorry, Mother," Peggy said

meekly. "It was very wrong."

"I know you are a high-spirited girl," Mistress Van Brundt said. "And I don't want you to feel as though you must live penned up in the house like a chicken in its coop."

"Yes, Mother."

"However—" Mistress Van Brundt paused. "You will not be allowed to leave the farmyard for the next week."

Peggy sat up straighter. She couldn't wait a whole week to help Frederick! "But, Mother, the soldiers are leaving now!" she protested. "The battle is over!"

"Yes, and if you had not disobeyed me earlier you would be free to go where you choose. But you left the yard despite my warnings. And you very nearly cost your father his life!"

"I am so sorry," Peggy said again. Hot

tears rolled down her cheeks. She was more miserable than she had ever been. Not only had she caused her parents pain, but she had also let down poor Frederick.

But she had no other choice. She could not disobey her mother again. She would wait one week. Then she would return to the burned-out barn. If Frederick was still there—*if* he was still *alive*—maybe she could help him somehow.

THE SEVEN DAYS PASSED slowly, even though Peggy had plenty of extra chores to do. She couldn't stop worrying about Frederick. She imagined him delirious with fever. She pictured British soldiers discovering him and dragging him away. Worst of all, she worried that he might have starved to death.

There was one bright spot in the long

week. Peggy and her family no longer had to worry so much about Willie and Jan. The boys had sent word through neighbors that they were safe. However, both of them had indeed joined the Continental Army.

Peggy lay awake each night, thinking about her brothers. In the room beside hers, she could hear her mother's muffled crying.

News of the Battle of Brooklyn was not good. It had been a terrible defeat for the colonists. Thousands of men had been killed in battle or died of illness or wounds in the days following. Many were taken prisoner. Almost an entire regiment from Maryland had drowned in the Gowanus marshes, not far from Peggy's house.

Luckily, General Washington and the last of his troops had made a dramatic escape during the night. Under cover of darkness, and with the help of the strong winds, they had slipped away in rowboats up the East River to Manhattan. Soon, they would retreat even further, into Westchester.

The week had brought another dramatic turn: Mister Van Brundt had decided to support the Patriot cause. Peggy was glad that he now accepted her brothers' decision to fight for freedom. She considered herself a Patriot now, too.

Peggy had plenty of time to think about the news that trickled into the farm as she waited out the week. At long last, her punishment ended. Once again she was free to roam the meadows and woods. During the last few days, she had gathered piece-by-piece a small bundle of things and hidden them under the mattress: a warm woolen blanket, a bowl and a chipped pitcher, some biscuits and cheese, and even the small end piece of a smoked ham.

On the first morning she was allowed out of the yard, Peggy gathered up the bundle and raced through the meadows to the old barn.

"Frederick?" she called from the doorway. There was no answer.

Peggy's heart dropped in her chest. Maybe he had run away. Or maybe the soldiers had found him after all!

Patches ran from the doorway to the corner of the barn and began to bark. Finally, Peggy heard a faint moaning sound.

"Frederick!" she cried again, hurrying to the corner of the barn. She spied the young man lying in the leaf pile. He was alive! Peggy sighed in relief. She saw that he was also very pale. He had grown a beard since she last saw him, too. Patches bounded over and licked his face.

"Peggy? That is you?" Frederick said. He had been sleeping. He looked up and smiled weakly.

"Yes, it's me. I'm so sorry I couldn't get away sooner," Peggy said. She began to unpack the bundle. "Here, I've brought some food. I'll go get some fresh water." She placed the ham and cheese and biscuits in front of Frederick in a small wooden bowl. Then she took the pitcher and hurried to the brook.

She returned with a full pitcher of water. Frederick took a long drink and then she helped him wash up a bit. To Peggy's relief, his fever seemed to be gone.

When Frederick seemed more comfortable, Peggy tried to explain about the battle and her brothers and what had happened at her house with the British soldiers. She wasn't sure he completely

understood her, but he nodded every once in a while and seemed pleased to listen. His condition was actually much better than Peggy had expected. His leg had begun to heal nicely, but he was still weak and very hungry.

"I'll be back tomorrow with more food," said Peggy. She pointed to the empty bowl.

"Thank you," said Frederick. "You are very kind. I am sorry that I am so much trouble to you."

"No trouble," Peggy said. "I hope you feel better soon." With that, she gently spread the blanket over him and left the barn.

Frederick reminded Peggy so much of her brothers. She hoped that if either of them was ever sick and in need of help, someone would be kind enough to help them, just as she was helping Frederick.

She didn't care if he *was* a spy.

She had decided not to mention anything about the sketchbook to him today. Perhaps Frederick was not a spy at all. Most likely, with his heavy German accent and broken English, he was a Hessian soldier. His coat appeared to be blue beneath all the dirt as well.

Perhaps Frederick had been wounded in some previous battle and been left behind by the British army. Or maybe he was even a deserter. He seemed like such a gentle person. Perhaps he did not want to fight anymore.

Tomorrow I will ask him some questions, Peggy told herself as she began to walk home through a meadow full of daisies, cornflowers, and wild carrot. She was watching Patches chase a butterfly when she saw a group of British soldiers in bright red coats step out of the woods into the meadow. There was no way of avoiding them. They had seen her before she saw them. Peggy's heart began to race.

"You there!" called one of the men, striding toward her. "What are you doing?"

"I'm going home," Peggy said.

"Pray tell, why are you walking so far from the house? And what brings you out here all alone?" demanded the soldier. He certainly seemed suspicious. Could he know about Frederick? Had he seen her go into the old barn?

Peggy thought fast. "I was chasing my dog," she said. "He runs away quite often. I have to go after him or he wanders off. I was afraid he might get lost."

"Well, he's not lost now," said the soldier. "Get back to your home quickly, miss. It isn't safe to be out walking alone these days."

"Yes, sir," Peggy said, giving a quick curtsy. "Thank you for warning me." She hurried away across the meadow and did not look back.

All the rest of the way home, she worried about those soldiers. Had they continued walking across the field? Or had they turned and followed the trail through the woods to the old barn? She would just have to wait and find out tomorrow. Right now she had no choice but to get home.

9

THE NEXT DAY, PEGGY MADE ANOTHER trip through the fields to the woods. She kept a sharp lookout for British soldiers this time.

Just in case anyone met her on her way to visit Frederick, Peggy had stuffed the food she was smuggling to him into her pockets. She had even tied her apron over her dress so that the bulges in her pockets wouldn't show.

Patches ran on ahead as always, and Peggy jogged along to keep up. She could feel the apples and chunks of cheese and bread she'd brought bouncing in her pockets as she ran.

Today she would tell Frederick about finding his sketchbook. Maybe she could discover whether he was indeed a spy by watching his reaction when she told him that British soldiers had seized the book.

It's too bad that Willie and Jan aren't here, Peggy thought once again. If Frederick *was* a spy, then they would surely know what to do. She sighed. Her brothers were busy now, helping General Washington prepare for the next battle. She was on her own.

"Get a torch!" Peggy suddenly heard a voice shout. She was so startled that she nearly jumped out of her skin. Something was going on at the old barn!

Peggy crept around in the bushes so that she wouldn't be seen. Finally, she saw them: The British soldiers she had met the day before had returned!

The men were knocking over parts of the remaining barn walls. One was bringing a lighted torch to the dark corner of the barn where Peggy had left Frederick. Was he still there? She couldn't tell.

Carefully she moved to get a better view. She held Patches close and prayed that he wouldn't bark this time. It was impossible to be sure, but it looked as if the barn was empty except for the soldiers.

"Someone has been here, all right," one of the soldiers was saying. "And not long ago, either." In disgust, he kicked at the leaf pile where Frederick had been sleeping.

Another soldier picked up the water pitcher Peggy had left behind. He examined it and threw it carelessly behind him. "No doubt it was one of those Colonial deserters resting up before running away. It is little wonder that they are no match for the King's men in battle. Cowards!"

A few of the other soldiers nodded. "Do you suppose the family up in the farmhouse knew they had a guest?" one of them asked. "Shall we question them?"

Peggy gulped as she crouched even lower in her hiding place. *Not again!* she thought.

"I think not," answered the soldier who seemed to be in charge. "Our deserter must have acted alone. There's nothing here but that broken water pitcher. No food, no clothing. And look, there is blood on these leaves. No, if there had been help from the farmhouse we would see some sign." Peggy sighed with relief.

"Let's move on," called out the soldier. "We may be able to track this scoundrel and hang him before nightfall."

Peggy shuddered. *Poor Frederick!* For a moment she wondered if the soldiers would set the barn on fire. Luckily, they gave up their search, put out the torch, and left the barn.

For a long time Peggy was afraid to move. She barely breathed. She waited until she was absolutely sure that no soldiers were coming back. Then, very cautiously, she emerged from her hiding place and took a quick look around the corner of the barn where Frederick had been hiding. The soldiers were right. There was nothing there.

"Where could he have gone?" Peggy asked herself. Now she would never know

if the mysterious young man was a spy, a runaway soldier, or just a lost traveler.

Peggy felt very disappointed. She wished she could know about Frederick. But most of all, she wished she had been able to help him more. Patches was sniffing all over the leaves that the soldiers had scattered around the floor. Then he began sniffing toward the doorway. He followed the trail outside, and Peggy hurried after him.

"Can you find Frederick, Patches?" Peggy asked. "Good boy!" She followed the little dog as he sniffed the trail that Frederick had left behind. As they headed along a familiar path through the woods, Peggy realized that Frederick must have gone back to the brook. Maybe he would still be there!

She ran quickly, with Patches following

her now. When they reached the clearing, Peggy looked around eagerly. But there was no one in sight.

"Of course he wouldn't be here," Peggy said with a sigh. "It would be much too dangerous for him. I should have known."

She walked across the clearing and went to sit in her favorite spot. The sun was streaming through the leaves. Birds were chirping. The brook babbled. Her special place was as pretty as ever, but somehow it wasn't the same. Sadly, Peggy lay back on the mossy bank and watched as Patches began to paw at a large rock.

"That's strange," Peggy said, sitting up again. "I don't remember ever seeing that rock before."

Patches began to paw faster.

"What have you got there, boy?" Peggy asked. Now the dog was digging and tugging at something under the rock. Peggy went over to investigate.

She couldn't believe her eyes. "Why, it's my sketchbook!" she cried. It was indeed her very own notebook that she had lent to Frederick.

Peggy rolled the rock away and uncovered the book. The stub of charcoal was stuck inside between two pages as always. Quickly, she opened it—and found a new sketch of her sitting with Patches! Underneath, in Frederick's fancy handwriting, were the words T-H-A-N-K Y-O-U, in English.

"Patches, look!" Peggy held out the page and the dog sniffed it eagerly. "This means Frederick must have escaped from those soldiers after all."

Peggy took another long look at Frederick's sketch. Suddenly, she knew what she'd been doing wrong whenever she tried to draw Patches. Had he been trying to help *her?*

She picked up the charcoal, sat down on the bank again, and turned to a new page in the book. "Patches, hold *still*," she said. "This time I am going to draw your ears right."

10

FOR ONCE, PEGGY WAS IN NO HURRY TO get home. She even stopped to pick a bunch of wildflowers along the way. She was so happy that Frederick had gotten away.

She was glad for another reason, too. This summer had been long and hard, but she felt sure that the worst was over in Brooklyn. She looked forward to the time when the war would be over and her brothers would come home. Then she could tell them the tale of the mysterious young man she had met in the woods. Patches gave a sharp bark. Peggy glanced toward her family's farmhouse and saw the British lieutenant's horse in the yard. "Oh, no!" she cried. "Not again!" She threw down her flowers and ran to the house. What kind of trouble was there now? What did that awful man want?

"Mother?" she called as she entered the house.

"Ah, here is the young maid I was looking for," said the lieutenant. He was standing just inside the doorway.

Peggy stopped in her tracks and looked from her mother to the lieutenant. The British officer had been looking for *her?*

"I have come to return your little souvenir to you," said the lieutenant. With a smile, he held out Frederick's sketchbook and offered it to Peggy.

"Oh, thank you," Peggy breathed gratefully. Perhaps even British soldiers could be kind sometimes.

"It appears to be the work of an earnest but rather uninteresting artist," the lieutenant said. "We have no further use for it. Apparently the lad was a painter. Those notes in the margins describe colors and pigments and such. Perhaps he planned to paint the things that he was sketching when he returned home. *If* he returned," the officer added under his breath.

"Then he wasn't a spy?" Peggy asked hopefully.

The lieutenant cleared his throat. "Most likely he was a Hessian deserter," he said. "And no, it appears he was not a spy. But one cannot be too careful in time of war. Good day, ladies."

With a nod, the lieutenant tipped his tricornered hat and turned to leave. Peggy stayed in the parlor while Mistress Van Brundt walked him outside.

So young Frederick was a painter! But Peggy had a feeling there was more to the matter than the British lieutenant had thought. Frederick had been afraid of being discovered; that much was certain. And what about the terrible wound on his leg? In her heart, Peggy was sure that Frederick's story was somehow more heroic and important than his sketchbook could reveal.

"What a lovely little book," said Mistress Van Brundt, eyeing the sketches as Peggy flipped through the pages once again.

"Yes," said Peggy, nodding. "Perhaps I will try to copy his drawing of our house. Or maybe this one of the brook."

"How fortunate that you found a book of

drawings, Margaret Anne," said Mistress Van Brundt with a smile. "It suits you so much better than a spy's book would have."

Peggy smiled back. Her mother had no inkling of how wrong she was about *that!* She, Peggy, had been doing quite a bit of spying these days. But it was nice to see her mother smiling again. Maybe someday she would tell her the real story behind the sketchbook. But not yet. For now it would be Peggy's secret.

Later that night, as she put Frederick's sketchbook away and got ready for bed, Peggy wondered if she would ever see the mysterious young man again. Perhaps he would return someday to see her. Then she could give him back his book and he could take it home.

But for now she and Patches would keep it safe and sound in Brooklyn.

HISTORICAL POSTSCRIPT

PEGGY VAN BRUNDT'S ENCOUNTER with the Hessian deserter on her family's Brooklyn farm did not actually happen. The Van Brundt family did not exist; however, many Dutch-American families like theirs lived through the American Revolution and the Battle of Brooklyn and watched British and Hessian soldiers roam their farmland.

In New York, July 4, 1776, Patriot General George Washington ordered the Declaration of Independence be read aloud at a public meeting to celebrate the Continental Congress's vote for independence. This boost to the colonists' morale could not have come at a better time. Just days before, 127 ships carrying British soldiers had landed on Staten Island to prepare for possible battles in New York. British General William Howe believed the colonists had some legitimate gripes and had hoped the colonists could resolve their differences with King George III. But the only offer of peace the crown made to the colonists was for those who would pledge their support to the King. This was not acceptable to the colonists, and as a result, General Howe was forced to attack.

However, General Howe was in no hurry to begin a battle because he knew more troops from Britain were on their way. General Washington, unsure of where an attack would come, divided his soldiers between Manhattan Island and Brooklyn. The number of General Howe's troops in the area increased greatly on August 22, when more British and Hessian troops landed off the coast of Gravesend Bay. The Hessians, like Frederick, were soldiers and allies of Britain who had been hired by King George III to help stop the rebellious colonists. They were called Hessians because the majority of them came from the two German principalities of Hesse-Cassel and Hesse-Hanau, which contributed 8,000 of nearly 22,000 soldiers who fought on behalf of the British. In comparison, General Washington commanded only 10,000 men total.

Some of the Hessians were called "deserters," because they ran away from the British camps and the battles. Unhappy fighting in a violent conflict, many chose to escape to the German settlements in Pennsylvania. Frederick was a typical deserter who risked death by the British because he did not want to fight the colonists.

The movement of Royal troops set up the Battle of Brooklyn on August 26, the day Peggy hurried home to her frightened parents when she heard gunfire. The British and Hessian attack on General Washington's forces came four days after General Howe's troops landed at Gravesend Bay. The Royal Army marched from the bay to the colonial position at what is known today as Flatbush, near Peggy's farmhouse. The Van Brundt family farm was in the area where the main battle took place, Gowanus and Bradford Pass, which is why the family members had so much contact with both British and Hessian soldiers. The Battle of Brooklyn was a resounding defeat for the colonial troops and General Washington as 1,000 of his troops were killed and as many captured. A regiment from Maryland lost so many soldiers in the Gowanus marshes that it could no longer be considered a useful unit.

General Washington immediately planned his retreat from Brooklyn. However, in order to deceive the British, he made it seem as if he would try to maintain control of Brooklyn Heights rather than leave Brooklyn altogether. Storms and heavy winds in the New York area after the battle on August 26 stopped the British from advancing north up the East River and attacking the colonists again. Bad weather also gave the colonists time to plan their retreat. Under a thick fog in the early morning of August 30, General Washington and his troops left Brooklyn.

The Colonial army first escaped to Manhattan, and then up the East River to Welfare Island (now known as Roosevelt Island), and then eventually further north to Westchester. Young men like Peggy's brothers, Willie and Jan, who joined the Colonial army after the Battle of Brooklyn, fought in five battles with the British in the New York area from September 15 through October 18, and then in the Battle of White Plains on October 28.

The Battle of Brooklyn is also known as the Battle of Long Island. Although Brooklyn sits geographically on Long Island, it has been incorporated as one of the five boroughs of New York City.